PULLING
Rapunzel's Hair

PULLING
Rapunzel's Hair

HONEY CUMMINGS

4 Horsemen
Publications, Inc.

Pulling Rapunzel's Hair
The Urban Erotica Fairy Tale Collection Book 8
Copyright © 2021 Honey Cummings. All rights reserved.

4 Horsemen Publications, Inc.
1497 Main St. Suite 169
Dunedin, FL 34698
4horsemenpublications.com
info@4horsemenpublications.com

Cover by 4 Horsemen Publications, Inc.
Typesetting by Autumn Skye
Edited by Heather Teele

Library of Congress Control Number: 2021951205

Audio ISBN: 978-1-64450-325-6
Ebook ISBN: 978-1-64450-326-3
Print ISBN: 978-1-64450-327-0

Table of Contents

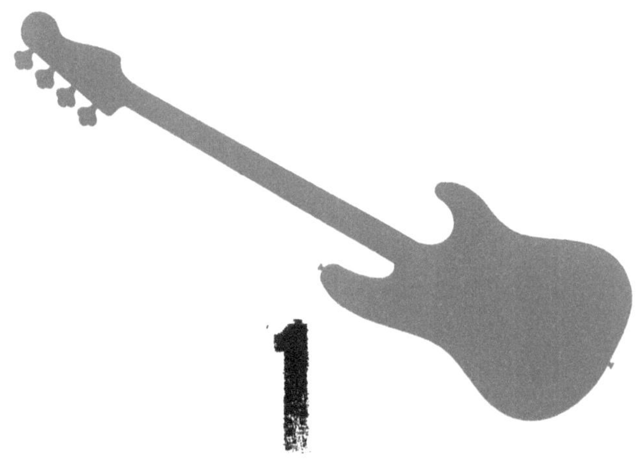

1

Rapunzel, Rapunzel

Rapunzel Ramone brushed a bleach-blonde-and-purple dread behind her shoulder before leaning back into her bass to continue tuning the instrument. *Red's Tavern* was still quiet, though the locals were coming in more steadily as Friday afternoon shifted into the evening hours. Being a freelance musician, she didn't belong to a particular band and rather enjoyed cherry-picking her nights and music as she saw fit. Tonight, she would be playing with a cover band that would satisfy her itch to play some classic rock for a change.

And maybe I can hook up with an out-rider afterward.

Glancing up, some college undergrads with goofy grins settled at a front table, and she rolled her eyes.

Not them. They can barely grow enough chin hair to shave each week. I need a manly man, someone who knows how to treat a girl and spoil her twice over. Enjoy the view, boys, because this is as close as you're getting to me.

They all loved to come and gawk at the curvy, tattoo-covered vixen who plucked on a bass. Tonight, she wore a thin tank top that did nothing to hide her purple bra, Edgar Allan Poe themed hand-sleeves, a plaid schoolgirl skirt with a studded black belt, fishnet thigh-high stockings with a hole over one knee, and black leather boots.

A smirk came to her face as she twisted the tuning peg. *Yup, every man's wet dream, complete with dreads—that's me. Granted, I'm only scantily dressed because the cam lights bake the fuck out of me on this damn stage. Wonder when Red will take Bob's advice and get them changed out or add a minisplit air conditioner to blow down cool air. A tanning bed is more forgiving than these tiny bastards.*

"Rapunzel, right?" The deep rumbling voice sent a chill up her spine as she turned to the lead singer, Jasper Holden. "You're my stand-in bassist tonight?"

"Yeah, Red called me and said you guys were in a pinch." Rapunzel stood, slung her bass behind her, and exchanged a firm handshake. *Shit, my hand feels tiny in his. He could be a stunt double for Bradley Cooper. Damn.*

The lead singer had an amazing voice; she had seen them play once before, and Rapunzel couldn't wait to hear if he continued to impress or if she was just too drunk to care that night. He stood at about 5'10", a few inches taller than her even with her boots on. He wore an old Metallica shirt three times too big with the arms and sides cut open and scruffy jeans to complete the old rock-n-roll bad boy ensemble.

That shirt swamps him; he looks like a kid wearing his big bro's shirt. Ha!

Jasper ogled her from head to toe before arching a brow. "They didn't tell me they were getting me a gorgeous punk-rock-princess in place of old Bob."

"Old Bob?" Rapunzel gave a sheepish grin. "As in Bob Pinkerton?"

"Yeah, you know Bob?" he marveled.

"He's taught me everything I know. Is he okay?" It was hard to tell if her heart was racing from Jasper or the idea that something could have happened to her precious mentor. "He's not in the hospital, is he?"

"Oh no, no, nothing like that." Jasper's face flushed, and he rubbed the back of his neck. "He's in Florida on vacation, and well, honestly, we completely forgot we needed a bassist for the next two weeks."

"Rather dangerous," she snorted, enjoying the red in his cheeks as his hazel eyes darted away in shame. "Two weeks, huh? Hope this is the only gig."

"Well, that's my next question for you." He inhaled deeply and puffed his cheeks out a moment as the bar grew noisy and guests claimed the last few tables. "We've got a few more shows until he gets back, and we were wondering if you're available…"

Rapunzel put her hands on her hips and pressed, "But you haven't even heard me play."

"Look, anyone taught by Bob must be pretty good." His eyes shot to the neck of her bass. The five o'clock shadow on his chin made his jawline more prominent and her heart raced. "And I can tell you know how to tune and play. A hobbyist doesn't drop the cash for a pink and gold Ibanez like that because they can. You only do that when you can play, show it off, and earn the money back fast and hard."

She bit her lip in thought and with a wide grin offered, "Okay, Jasper. If you like my playing tonight, and," Jasper met her gaze on the pause and she continued, "I have a good time tonight, I'll consider it."

He narrowed his eyes at her, sucking on his cheek before agreeing. "Okay. I can do that. Definitely will make sure you have a good time tonight no matter what."

"Promise?" She winked and slung her bass back into her hands, plucking a riff from *Seven Nation Army.* "I'm hard to please."

"I might surprise you, your Majesty." Winking back at her, he spun to the mic and switched it on. "Are you ready to get this show poppin' tonight?"

The bar roared and whistled with their drinks raised high, lights brightened on the stage, and the audience faded into darkness. Rapunzel glanced back to see the drummer ripping through his set to get more out of the patrons. The lead guitarist jumped in, and she was hot on their heels, earning a '*damn girl*' expression from Jasper. His grin widened and again her heart fluttered as his deep voice rolled across the room over the speakers.

At least Red's has great acoustics— Rapunzel's thoughts halted as Jasper began singing "Pour Some Sugar on Me" by Def Leppard. *Holy shit, the man can sing! Being on stage, I can hear it sans-mic and… oh, I think I'm going to wet my panties.*

Shooting a look across the bar, Red locked eyes with her and lipped, *He can sing!*

The guitar and drums thumped through the speakers; the volume of the music vibrated through her lungs, getting her blood pumping and adrenaline climbing. She stomped across the stage, bouncing to the beat of the song as the bar began to clap. The lead guitar ripped through the solo, adding a bit of creative flair to it and bringing a smile to her face. Jasper's part followed and he spun to her, leaning in as he began the next chorus.

"*You got the peaches, I got the cream…*"

♫ Rapunzel, Rapunzel ♫

Rapunzel's face reddened as those bright hazel eyes caught her gaze. His smirk widened, and she spun to lean into him. The bar whistled as Rapunzel wiggled her ass and dipped down before they broke apart.

A chill of arousal tingled up her spine. *That was too thick to be the microphone wire. Holy shit! Someone is quick to reply to that little hip shake.*

The song ended and he called the next set back to them, "Kickstart My Heart."

Shit, going hard and heavy with old school metal! I'm digging this… Motley Crüe, here I come!

Again, the bar began popping, singing along, but Jasper's voice rose above the cacophony of nostalgic drunks. The music brought more and more patrons into the club as the last strips of daylight stopped flashing through the opening door. A whole gang of bikers stood at the pool tables, too distracted to play a full round.

This man is worthy of being a siren with the way he catches everyone's attention! Even Tex is enjoying himself.

Rapunzel and Jasper could feel the reaction of the audience enjoying their shenanigans. The game of tit-for-tat from playful body rubs and ever-braver gropes between them seemed to fill the air with a sexual charge.

"…a lady with a body from outer space."

Van Halen's "Runnin' with the Devil" slowed the room down and gave everyone a moment to catch a breath. Rapunzel's heart thudded in her chest, fingers and arms aching from the tension of playing hard. Sweat trickled down the divot of her back. Looking at Jasper, as sweat dripped from his chin and locks of hair plastered to his forehead, made Rapunzel's heart skip a beat.

I wonder if he sweats that much while—what the hell am I thinking? What a horny harlot I am tonight! But really, do I dare sleep with the lead singer? How cliché… She watched as he sang to the audience and paced on stage. *Well, it's not a habit, and he's singing and working the stage as good as any pro…*

Rapunzel blushed as Jasper continued serenading her in his rock-metal ballad. The last time she had lost herself to this kind of music had to be when she went to see *KISS* live. Each stolen glance was clueing her in on key lyrics.

"Got nobody waiting at home…"

Laughing, Rapunzel was picking up on exactly what Jasper was doing, or in this case, messaging to her. *This crazy man is picking songs to let me know he wants to hook up, isn't he? All this eye-fucking and rubbing on each other. Clever man. Can't deny it's sort of hot!* The song shifted, and he took a swig of his water by the drummer before returning to the stage.

"How we doing tonight?"

The crowd roared, a few folks dropping cash in the tip jar on the stage's edge. "Keep bringing those tips, and we'll keep bringing the jams. One more song and we're gonna take a break to cool down." Jasper turned back to the band and whispered, "Princess of the Dawn." He licked his teeth and winked at Rapunzel.

Goosebumps rolled across Rapunzel's skin. *I haven't played this song since practicing with Bob. Not just anyone knows this fantasy-fueled memento of old school metal.*

The band played it slower, and she skillfully adjusted. *He's challenging my skills.* She locked eyes and his leg bounced in the slower tone as the riff started, the build exciting and agonizing. *I love this song…* Jasper sang the first line, deep and haunting unlike any version she'd heard before. He had made the song his, and now his rough, thunderous voice made her weak in the knees.

"…her kiss is bittersweet…"

Rapunzel leaned into him once more, his cock hard under the shirt and jeans, pressing against her ass cheeks. Her breath caught, fingers threatening to fumble on the neck of her bass guitar. An arm snaked between her and the bass, pulling her into the hard planes hidden under his clothes. Jasper took the heat up another level, grinding gently against her, promising what he'd rather be doing at this moment before turning away as the song ended. Rapunzel watched him leave with hungry eyes as she dropped her stare. Jasper's shirt was too long for anyone to see what she had firmly felt.

Exactly how big and worked up did you get on stage grinding on me?

The drummer and lead guitarist ended the last notes, and the race between Rapunzel unstrapping her bass and Jasper sliding the microphone into the stand began. Her hair caught the neck of her bass, and she muttered every curse trying to untangle it. The bar erupted into a roar of voices, laughter and the clinking of glasses commenced the intermission.

Jasper had disappeared.

Shit. I was hoping for some intermission fun, but…

Let Down Your Hair To Me

Flustered and heart racing, she squinted at the crowd. Through the surge of people placing tips and song suggestions in the glass jar or rushing the bar for drinks, she couldn't see where Jasper had disappeared. The lead guitarist blocked her way off stage, insisting he shake her hand. Shaking her head—she hadn't heard the words he said to her—she gave a haphazard smile.

"I'm sorry." She pointed to her ears. "Say that again—I didn't hear you."

"I said," he inhaled deeply and projected his words to her, "that was great playing!"

She laughed, shaking his hand firmer. "I appreciate that. Granted, I have to say, you guys work well together, and that makes it easier to fall in line."

"I'd dare to say that you're better than Bob!" His eyebrows rose high, his voice deep and throaty like Sam Elliot; he could pass for his younger brother. "The name's Chad. Please tell me you'll be joining us for the next few shows until the old coot comes back from his vacation."

"Ah, you know, Jasper was trying to convince me of that too…" Her voice trailed off as she looked through the crowd for the lead singer. "Speaking of which, where did he go?"

Chad, being so tall, peered over her and shrugged. "Not sure. Getting a drink, out back for fresh air, or might be taking a piss."

Of course. What else is there to do in a bar between sets? Rapunzel snorted. "Th-thanks. Well, we'll see how the whole band feels about my skills by the end of the night, if I can keep up with a rowdy group of boys like you all."

He scoffed, chortling. "You give me too much credit. We don't get shit-faced like in our green years. Not into the groupies, no energy to keep up with them."

Smirking, Rapunzel teased, "Then you should tell that to old Bob."

"Bob has a sex drive like no other," guffawed Chad. "One day he might find a gal that can keep up. I still can't believe he hosted an orgy at his place a while back."

"I'm pretty sure he's at a nude resort or beach at this very moment!" Laughing,

Rapunzel patted Chad's arm and slipped past him off the stage.

Again, she spun around looking for Jasper only to find her view blocked by a wall of college undergrads. *These gawkers from the front table, ugh!* She frowned, recognizing them as the crew who had whistled and heckled her during the first set. Taking a step to cut through an opening, she found it closed quickly. *Shit! Not this again…*

"Hey good lookin'," cooed the backward cap undergrad. "We were wondering what you were doing after the show."

"Um, look boys, I appreciate the playful banter, but I'm working—"

They all took a closer step to her, and she became very aware that she was cornered. She was stuck in a dark nook, too far to shout to the stage; the only escape was the men's restroom behind her.

Time to initiate the "mom voice" to see if I can push these jackals off. I am not in the mood for this bullshit tonight.

Clearing her throat, she shifted to a stiffer pose and raised her voice. "Look, I'm working. I'm not here to pick up a date."

"So, after you're off work, you're coming to hang out with us, right?" offered the pock-faced friend.

"No," Rapunzel's voice carried a stern chill to it. "I'm not going anywhere with you three."

Another step forward forced her to bump her back against the men's door, making it open slightly. *Dammit, every man I trust in this place is out of shouting range and pisses out in the parking lot like a dog.* Her hand gripped the door's edge, keeping it from closing. *If this gets bad, I am not against locking myself in the shitter and shrieking like a banshee.*

"Oh c'mon," he whined, making a pouty face. "Look, we'll buy you drinks, and we got a whole liquor cabinet at the house, baby doll."

"Don't call me that," she replied flatly.

"Guys, this is going too f—" They shoved the third friend who shot her a pitiful expression.

Rapunzel cocked her head. "Look, you're making me uncomfortable. Back up and get out of my way."

"Say please," the pock-faced undergrad licked his lips, eyes dipping provocatively before whispering to her, "Or we can save the begging for when I'm behind you—"

"HEY!" Chad's booming voice made everyone jolt, and the third grad walked away from the stage.

Oh shit, their friend saved me!

"WHAT THE FUCK YOU TWO DOING WITH MY BASS PLAYER?"

Thank you, Chad, for—

A hand gripped her wrist, pulling here into the men's bathroom. The door shut hard behind her. The force of the thud took. A hand reached behind her and flipped the lock. The man had her pinned between him and the door, her arms above her head as he leaned in over her to listen. Looking up, she saw Jasper staring down at her, his brow furrowed with worry. Blinking a few times, Rapunzel's heart skipped a beat.

I feel like I just stole a moment with my high school crush. Am I really into him this much?

"You okay?" he murmured down to her.

"Now I am." She shrugged. *I want to ask him to back away, but some part of me is enjoying how close we are… wait…* "Have you been in here the whole time?"

He pulled away, freeing her. "Y-yeah." His face flushed red before he spun his back to her. "I uh…"

Rapunzel gave a sheepish expression, able to see his face in the mirror. *He's embarrassed… did he… no… it couldn't be?* "Did you come in here to…"

His eyes met hers in the mirror, widening as he bit his lip.

"…unload?" Now she was beaming at the idea, recalling how hard he felt rubbing against her on the stage. "You know, clear the pipes so-to-speak?"

Jasper cringed, closing an eye before confessing, "I can't exactly control that I'm very attracted to you, and well, the body knows what it wants before I do."

"I can't lie…" Rapunzel walked to the vanity and pulled herself onto it, legs swinging. "It was turning me on too. Not that I make a habit of sleeping with band members either."

"Look, I don't want you to think I'm that douchebag who has to go around sleeping with the female band members or fucking groupies in the back alley." He seemed on the defense, marching into the single stall and flushing the toilet, making her snicker. "So, yeah, I'm not that type either so… I didn't mean to go too far on stage…"

She scoffed. "I didn't say you were."

Jasper leaned on the stall door, his lips twisted as he looked her over. "Enough about my cock—what was happening out there?"

"College dirtbags." Again, she shrugged but looked away with a sense of insecurity. "I was handling it."

He snorted, walking closer, his finger gentle under her chin to lift her eyes to his. "It's okay to scream if you want. That's more than enough to spook anyone who aims to do you harm."

"The only screaming I want to do," Rapunzel's voice came out in a sultry tone as she gripped Jasper's shirt, tugging his ear to her lips, "is when I get you all alone to myself."

His hand rode up her legs, snaking under her skirt, as he cooed, "In that case, we're all alone right now." Hot lips began to blaze a trail down her neck and shoulder. "I might have ruined my chances for some fun…" Jasper squeezed her thigh before rubbing her underwear and teasing her pussy through the thin fabric. "…but I don't see why I can't make you feel better."

Rapunzel moaned, "You're a tease."

"Maybe." His finger pushed the fabric to the side, sliding between the folds and making her gasp. "Have I mentioned I'm really good with my fingers?" Slick with her wetness, they slid back up to her swollen clit and she inhaled swiftly. "Aren't we worked up?"

"I told you, I—" She struggled to get the words out as her knees squeezed tight on his hips where he stood. "Dammit that feels… so good." Her body arched and Jasper began kissing at her neck as she whimpered. "So close…" she huffed.

"You going to cum for me? Hmm?" His voice rumbled low as his finger slid down again and dipped inside her, stroking slow as her pussy squeezed tight around him. "Cum for me, baby."

"Oh, oh so close… don't stop," she panted, gripping the edge of the counter.

Jasper pulled his finger over the span and once more began circling her pink jewel. Rapunzel's legs shook with the rising pleasure. Her hands white-knuckled, she clung to her perch. Her breath caught, and he slowed the motion, making her moan.

"You know you want to cum." The heat of his breath washed over her neck, adding to her arousal. "I want to make you cum. Are you going to let me make you cum?"

Rapunzel's heart fluttered, the dirty talk adding to the erotic moment, something she hadn't experienced before. "Y-yes…" It was hard to talk as she tried to relax, to allow herself and her body to indulge in his touch. "I want to cum for you."

He nuzzled her neck and sucked on it. She tilted her hips, and he dipped his fingers inside a few more times, stroking her. Moaning, she rocked against the motion of his hand. The fingers retreated and a more aggressive onslaught with two fingers made her yelp.

"So close…" she whimpered, eyes shut tight as she teetered on the edge, the sensation agonizing. "I want to cum for you…"

Jasper nibbled at her neck and began to moan like he too would cum. "Come for me, baby."

"Y-yes… just… a little…"

The orgasm hit her hard, and she kicked and bucked.

A swift inhale and jolt of her body made him change course. Fingers stroked hard and fast, making her squeal in ecstasy. As his stroking slowed, she came back to earth and looked him in the eyes.

"I've never cum like that before." Heartbeat racing, she panted from the mountainous release he had brought her with his fingers.

Chuckling, he pulled away to start washing his hands. "Well, that's only the appetizer. We keep running around on stage like that, and you might need to give me a hand next break someplace more private."

"I think I can return the favor." She slid off and took a moment to find her legs again. "Give me a moment before we sneak out."

I can't believe I've got baby deer legs from him playing with me like that. Wonder how well he can work that massive single digit he's hiding in his pants…

3

A King's Son

Jasper peeked out of the bathroom door first, waving her out as she darted for the bar. All she could think is how desperately she needed a drink. *I can't believe we just did that. I've never had a man finger me until I came like that, and when he moaned on my neck…* A shudder shook her as her skin dimpled. *So, fucking hot.* Red was quick to open a bottle of Yuengling and slide it to her.

"You okay?" Red raised an eyebrow. "You look a little … flushed."

"Just overheating some…" Taking down half the bottle, her lips popped, and she inhaled as if coming up to the surface for air. "Hey, next break, can uh, can I use your office to talk business with Jasper?"

"Business or pleasure?" Red leaned on the bar, watching as Rapunzel's face reddened. "Darling, if that energy on stage is just the tip of the iceberg, I say kudos and feel free to unload next break… literally." With a wink, Red rushed to help another customer.

Best wing man ever.

Downing the last half of her liquid courage, she headed for the stage as the band started to settle back into position. Chad gave her a nod and pointed with his chin. The table where the college dirtbags had sat was now occupied by some giggling housewives having a girls' night out.

Phew, I guess the bouncer Peter sent those assholes packing! They were cackling loudly, whistling at Jasper, and gobbling him up with their hungry eyes. Another look, and Rapunzel shuddered. *Isn't this just replacing one form of harassment with another? And who will save Jasper if Grandma's harlot crew corner him by the bathroom?*

Jasper stiffened his posture, giving her a large span to walk by, as if he'd decided to give her bigger boundaries. *No, don't do that! I'm totally into you. Forget about Granny and the old farts! I will not let them squash what I have going on—what happened in that bathroom was amazing!*

The energy Jasper had started with drained from him with each cat call as if he was afraid to release any form of sexual attraction in the gapping jowls of the harpies in the front row. When he stumbled on a lyric, Rapunzel shot him a bewildered look. That's when she saw it, the same look she had on her face in the first set at one point and decided it was time to act.

I can't watch this farce go on any longer. Who knew some retirees could make Mr. So-bold-I-just-jerked-myself-and-her-off-in-a-public-bathroom cower on stage! He saved me, so time to save him!

She sidestepped in front of Jasper to block his line of sight to the table of feral cougars, leaning back into him like they had done during the first set. His entire body, tense and hard as a wall, took a moment to react to the way she slid up and down him. The onlookers whistled as Rapunzel wiggled her ass into him, the familiar rise in his pants egging her on as he pulled her into him. *That's it. He's starting to relax and focus on me now.* Together they dipped down, earning another wave of cheers as he sang the lyrics with newfound vigor, and she shouted into the mic with him.

"*Shook me all night long!*"

And now the whole bar was shouting along with them.

Chad leaned into the solo, and Rapunzel marched up to him, her dreads swaying to the beat as she plucked to mirror him. Jasper leaned into the mic stand, getting his groove back. He shot a look her way, grinning wide. Rapunzel laughed, shaking her head as she focused on the riffs and returned to her spot on stage.

There we go. Got him back on track!

The song ended and he spun to the little table by the drummer, guzzled down a bottle of water, and poured the last bit over his head. The cam lights overhead rained heat down on them, and there were more songs to choose from. He dipped into the jar of slips, looking over a few before nodding his head at one in particular and dropping the unchosen back into the fray.

He flashed the paper to the crew, then to Rapunzel: "Unskinny Bop" by Poison. Reaching out, Rapunzel gripped his wrist and pulled him close enough to whisper in private.

"Hey, I don't know this one," she whispered in earnest.

"You've got a good ear. The bass in this one is basic. I mean, you know one Poison song, you've played them all." He leaned into her ear. "The lyrics may remind you of our fun in the bathroom."

Pushing him back, she laughed, face red. "Fine, but if I play like shit, it's your fault."

"A price I will gladly pay!" The music began and he locked eyes with her, singing the provocative lyrics with a playful smirk on his face.

Rapunzel took a few stumbles until she finally caught a signal in the drums to aid her. Chad shook his head approvingly, impressed how the fumbling was hidden from untrained ears. Jasper was back to teasing and grinding her from behind.

How the hell no one see this giant cock in his pants under that baggy shirt is beyond me!

The whole bar was jamming, and after a few more songs, they were glad to hit the next break. Sweat dripped from Jasper's chin, and she set her bass down, leaning it on the back wall. They were all breathless and glad to escape the stage's heat lamps.

Glancing at the audience, she flinched. The flock of harpies were coming for the stage exit, or rather, coming for Jasper. Rapunzel, startled, half-ran to catch up with her precious lead singer. Gripping his wrist, she pulled on him and found herself jerked backward, unable to budge or lead him anywhere. He gave her a baffled expression as he stood like an anchor.

"Where are you taking me?" he mused with a sparkle in his eyes.

She glanced over his shoulder at the old cougars stalking ever closer. "I'm trying to save you…" Clearing her throat and giving him a serious, low-brow expression. "Let's go talk about my pay in the office. You owe me for this last-minute request."

"The office … about the request?" Catching the licking lips of one of the grannies, he let her pull him through the crowd. "Yes!" He was shoving her forward now, talking loudly. "Let's go discuss payment." He smirked, chortling. "I owe you more than one night's worth of payments, don't I?"

"Damn straight you do." She pulled him through the office door, slamming it shut.

Now she found herself locking the door and pinning him there. *Wow, talk about a complete gender role flip from the last break session.* Granted, she was so small it seemed goofy and awkward. On the other side, they could hear the older women bickering amongst themselves.

"Dammit, Ethel," screeched the Harpy. "You spooked him!"

"I just wanted to give him a nickel for his pickle," hissed the cougar.

Patting Jasper's chest, Rapunzel smirked. "You totally owe me."

"I'll gladly owe you whatever you want if you keep pulling me out of danger like that." He leaned down, kissing her deeply as their tongues met before breaking away to add, "I kind of like being the damsel in distress."

"Stop." She turned away from him, but he pulled her back and wrapped his arms around her as his hands started wandering. "About that payment…"

I guess we'll be using the office for pleasure after all.

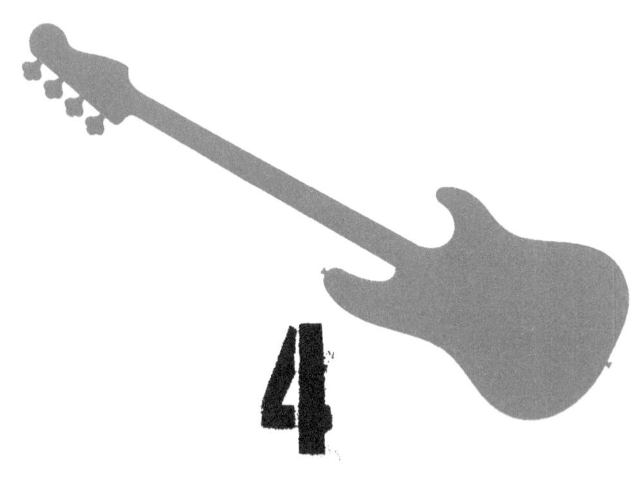

4

He Could
Have No Peace

Jasper's hand slid under her shirt, shoving her bra up so he could squeeze her breast. Rapunzel moaned, leaning into him where he teasingly grinded against her. He nuzzled and kissed her neck and shoulder, humming into her as his cock grew harder. His other hand glided downward, dipped beneath her skirt, and trailed downward until his finger graced her swollen clit. She inhaled as he began circling her jewel.

"I love the way you moan," his voice rumbled low into her ear.

Another gasp escaped her lips as Jasper pinched her nipple. His cock throbbed under his jeans against her. *He's so big, it sends shivers through me.* The heat of his body added to the arousal building at her core; the desire whispering in her mind: *Yes, touch me more, talk dirty to me with that sexy voice, and tease me with that…*

Fingers slid across her pussy, teasing that they might enter her at any moment. She spun around, her hands pulling him into her, clawing at his back to ensnare him. Rapunzel's body ran hot with passion. *I've never been so hungry for a man to fuck me.* Her fingers relaxed, gliding over the hard planes of Jasper's back and up across his shoulders until they tangled in his wet locks. Cold droplets shook loose and fell down on her skin. Dimples waved over her like ripples on a serene lake.

Teeth nibbled her ear, and she whimpered, "Talk dirty to me."

"Oh?" He snorted, the heat of it making her shudder in pleasure. "You're going to have to beg me for it."

"Please." She tilted her hip, and he coyly pulled away, still leaning in to nibble on her ear. "I want…"

Fingers teased the opening of her pussy, wet with anticipation. "You want me to dive into the deep end already, hmm?"

"Y-yes." With two fingers, he slid slow and agonizingly into her heat, and she arched into him.

"Have you been a good girl, Rapunzel?" A hard twist of her nipple and she gasped; her thighs squeezed against his hips as he pushed her onto the desk. "Hmm? Have you been a good girl? I'm waiting…"

"Oh…" Jasper started stroking in and out, slow as her pussy tightened around his digits. "I've been… b-been…"

"You've been what?" He mused before licking across her shoulder and up her neck. He whispered, "Tell me, have you been naughty or nice, Rapunzel?"

She tried to rock her hips to deepen his stroking, but he wouldn't lose the agonizing speed and depth, making her crave for more, for *rougher*. "I've been good!" she blurted at last.

Snickering, Jasper began picking up speed as his silken words blessed her ears. "What do you want for being such a good, good girl, hmm?"

"To be…" Another gasp took the words from her as his hand slid to her other breast to pinch the erect nipple. "I want… fuck…" She moaned as his wrist twisted and began rubbing her pussy in a new direction, her legs shaking with the slow rise of an orgasm. "I want... t-t-to be..."

"To be?" he cooed, pulling away from her as he began to open his pants. "Come on, I'm giving you a moment to catch your breath and tell me what you want so badly."

Rapunzel's heart pounded through her like a thousand horses racing with no end in sight. *I just melt when this man touches me and whispers in my ear... holy smokes, where has he been all my life!*

Swallowing, she willed herself to speak her desires. "I want to be naughty. I mean..." She spread her legs wider, her own fingers dipping between her folds. "I want you inside me."

Without Jasper so close, hidden away in her neck and dreads, his face turned red. As his zipper slid to rock-bottom, his cock stood at attention, the tip swollen and dripping from his own agonizing excitement. Biting her lips, Rapunzel slid off the desk and knelt before him, still playing with herself.

I owe him from last session, don't I?

A moan escaped him as her silken tongue ran hot across the underbelly of his cock. Through heavily lidded eyes, Jasper peered down at Rapunzel, meeting her gaze. Her plump lips cupped the tip of his cock where her tongue began circling. A shudder rattled through him, the erotic pleasure peaking as he watched her fingering herself as she pulled his length into her mouth.

"I'm doing everything I can to be a good boy." He now bit his bottom lip, his gaze never breaking.

She rocked back, her lips popping as they released his cock. "Oh? And what would we do if we were being a bad boy?"

He paused, searching her face a moment as she ran her tongue up and down his hardened length. "Grab you by the hair and fuck that dirty little mouth until I cum," he confessed, face flashing red. "But I don't think—"

"Do it," she dared him with a provocative tone as her tongue circled once more before pleading, "Teach me a lesson. Make me sing, bad boy."

He looked away, sucking on his cheek. A smirk crept on his face as his eyes came back to her in time for her to suck his dick back into her mouth. Her tongue wiggled and slid underneath, the suction pulling him deeper until the tip pressed firm against the back of her throat. Groaning, he reached down and gripped her ponytail, pulling Rapunzel's hair until she almost came off his cock. She smiled, tongue wagging up at him, before he slammed her forward and deeper onto him.

Her breasts jiggled as he repeated the motion a few times, occasionally allowing her to catch her breath. The heat of her panting rolled over his dick and added to how he teetered on the edge of cumming. Pressing back between her lips, she resisted slightly, eyes on his and smirking with rebellion. That look of indulgence, knowing that at any given moment she could take his pleasure away, excited him.

She moaned, her hands diving between her thighs as he fucked her mouth. Panting, he watched as her legs shook. She screamed but was muffled by his cock as her orgasm peaked. Pressing deep into her throat, he inhaled swiftly and moaned as he released. Tilting his head back, he grinded into her throat until his cock at last finished.

Hands pulled him back between plump lips; Rapunzel wasn't done with this blowjob just yet. *They're always super sensitive after they cum, so if I…*

He let go of her hair to steady himself on the desk. Hungry, she suckled, pulling, and pushing herself in and out on his dick. Jasper covered his mouth with the other hand, eyes rolling back with the wave of pleasure it brought. A grunt escaped him as he forcibly came again, leaving him aching.

She stood, giving him some hearty slaps on the shoulder before chuckling. "That's my thank you for what you did in the bathroom earlier."

"Oh?" His brows rose as he stood, riding out the wave of his own orgasm. "I don't think anyone has forced me to keep going after… well…" He lost his words as she licked her lips and shimmied off her panties. "What are you doing?"

"They're soaked." She chucked them in the trash can. "It's uncomfortable to wear wet panties, don't you agree?"

"I, uh," Clearing his throat, he stood straight and tucked himself away. "I suppose I can't argue with that. But are you sure you want to be on stage sans-panties like that?"

Spinning back, Rapunzel cupped his face and smiled. "You're assuming I haven't done that before. Cute." Patting his cheek, she giggled and opened the office door, adding with a wink, "I'll think over the payment, but I might need a little more. Let's bang out the details after this last set."

Definitely need to bang it out after the show. Standing tall, she strode out confidently, fluttering on the adrenaline of their secret moment. Another beer washed down his salty flavor, and they were back under the heat of the cam lights.

The Ladder into the Tower

The old hags at the front table had left. The bar was thinning out as people led by designated drivers stumbled toward the door. Now, the front door was propped open to let the cool night air in, and a flicker of headlights signaled another Guber driver or ride had come for its passenger. Jasper met her gaze, face flushing, before turning back to what remained of their audience.

"Last set for the night, folks. Be sure to tip the waitress and lovely owner, Red, there in the back. Closing time will be upon us shortly." Jasper held up a whiskey on the rocks, and a few regulars whistled and held up their drinks in turn. "So last call for alcohol for those thirsty or still needing some liquid courage!"

He took it down, shoulders shuddering as he placed it next to a fresh bottle of water on the stage table. Diving into the fishbowl of requests, he rifled through them. Chad started plucking the *Jeopardy* theme and Rapunzel joined in. At last, he glanced at the paper and flashed it at the rest of the crew, "Thunderstruck."

As they began the famous opening, the audience joined in, humming along with the band. They banged on the tables and stomped their feet to add to the thunderous beat of *THUN-DER;* everyone shouted the words in all their excitement.

The entire bar was all smiles as Jasper pitched his voice high enough to capture the song in all its glory.

"No help from you!" he sang, pointing at her, and everyone whistled.

The lyrics flew, adding to the expressions and tit-for-tat that unfolded. *Damn, dude. You need to get more blowjobs if this is how it unfolds on stage!*

He wobbled his knees, shaking them, and she turned away trying to keep her laughter from hitting the mic. Jasper pulled her back in time to announce the chorus more. At first, she shook her head in denial before nodding in agreement, and he let out a hissing, *"Yeah."*

Everyone sang loud and clear. The next song continued at the same level, closing the night with a strong set of old school rock and classics no one could resist joining. The energy popping through the place was like a grand finale of a firework display. They were down to the last two songs before the amazing night would be at its end.

Who knew tonight would be so incredible, so sexy…?

This time Jasper made the first move, a knee sliding between her thighs from behind. He lifted slightly, and she grinded her pussy against it and stiffened, leaning back into him. She bit her lip and lowered her brow at him but only got a knowing wink before he pulled away. Again, he surprised her that with each time he came near her, he could make her pulse flutter.

I want him to bend me over and fuck me on stage at this rate.

The songs began to wind down, but Jasper's moves grew bolder, and they seemed to be slow dancing with one another on stage. The creeping hard-on hidden under the oversized shirt added to how her loins throbbed with want.

Singing over her shoulder, the heat of his body and breath called forth those erotic moments in the bathroom and office.

Touch me and fuck me, baby. I'm all yours!

Jasper's hand slid over her hip, hidden from prying eyes behind her bass. His fingers trailed down the fabric of the skirt. Her body twitched against him, and she became very aware how muscled his body was, like a wall behind her. Squeezing her eyes tight, she tried to focus on the riff as he rubbed over her clit.

Did he read my mind?!

His cock firm against her ass, she wiggled and returned the motion, partially to bring relief from his fingers making it damn near impossible to play. As he groped her pussy, she struck the wrong chord. Jasper was gone as if it spooked him, and he was back at the mic stand trying not to laugh. Chad and the drummer were chuckling.

How dare he do that to me!

"Goose her again!" slurred someone from the bar top.

Jasper choked on the lyrics and the song fell apart. "Sorry boys, I don't know about you, but I want to make it back home in one piece."

A roar of laughter erupted, and the lights overhead began to flash before staying on. The whole place groaned. *Red's calling it. The signal has fired off to pay up and get the hell out.*

"Ah, looks like closing time. We'll be here next week and hope to see you then, folks!" A few whistle bursts and the crowd turned for the bar to tab out in one mass group. Jasper clunked the mic in place and leaned in to whisper to Rapunzel, "And I hope you follow me off this stage."

His hand grabbed her ass and a chill snaked up her spine. *At this rate, I will follow you and that monster cock anywhere, Mister Magic Fingers!*

Before she could say much, he was throwing cash at the drummer and lead guitarist. *We're done-done. Time to drop my shit in the case and toss it in Red's office. He's getting everyone out of the way for...*

Hustling, her body exhilarated with the anticipation to have one more round with Jasper. Her bass and things were shut tight in the case and the lock spun. Just off stage, Rapunzel locked eyes with Jasper. He motioned with a nod of his head for her to follow, and after a crowd of women obscured the gap between them, he was gone.

Rapunzel's heart fluttered. *Fuck, where did he go?*

Jumping off stage, she beelined for the office, and tossed it in. Part of her hoped to see him there at the desk waiting for her, but no one was there. Stepping back into the now nearly empty bar, the stage was bare, the band gone, and Red cashed out a few last regulars. Her heart leapt to her throat.

Did he just bail on me? Really? With that rock hard cock… no way.

6

I Will Try My Luck

whistle called her attention behind her where Jasper was slipping through the kitchen door. Her eyes locked with his and his smirk widened before she lost the connection. She gave chase. Weaseling through the last bit of crowd and chairs, she disregarded those who called out to her or tried to give her praise; she was going to catch her prey.

Rushing through the swinging door, ignoring the cook yelling for her to get out, she hurried through the back door. It thudded closed, the bar noise fell silent, and she found herself stumbling out into the back alley. She had lost him to the shadows of the night. Her skin pimpled as the cool air brought a round of shivers. Another whistle from a dark corner brought a smile to her face. Hips swaying, she paced herself.

Don't look desperate, don't look desperate...

"What's up with the game of chase?" she narrowed her eyes as a chill of arousal rolled through her. *I caught you!* "And all that touching and eye-play on stage... what are you hinting at, Bad Boy?" she teased.

Cheeks red, eyes lingering on her lips, he murmured, "I want to taste you so badly," before cupping his hand over his mouth as if trying to prevent anything else from slipping out. "I'm sorry, I don't usually rub up on… on female musicians. I don't know but something about you just has me all…" Holding his breath for a moment, he at last confessed, "…so fucking worked up."

Rapunzel pulled his hand down and kissed him. Lips parting, they deepened it as she pinned him between her and the brick wall. Tugging up his shirt, she wanted to feel his hard cock with her hand once more. She rubbed down the front of his tightened jeans and it throbbed. As she groped him, he moaned into her mouth, tilting his hip to press it firmer into her palm.

Pulling away, Rapunzel demanded, "Fuck me. Right now."

"Anything for her majesty." The deep coo sent an enthralling tremble through her.

Her fingers unfastened the button, and she licked her lips as she unzipped what she wanted the most. The heat of his hand slid under her tank top, shoving the cup of her bra up and off her breasts to grope her once more.

"I don't think I've ever fucked someone I barely met in a back alley." He searched her face, confusion and curiosity filling his expression.

Rapunzel laughed. "I think we're well met after the last few breaks and the way this felt against me."

Jasper wrapped his arms around her, pulling her to him and started to lick her nipple before drawing it between his lips. Her fingers were firm, stroking his length. Her pussy throbbed as her thumb slid over the tip of his cock, slick with pre-cum. Biting her lip, she arched into him, enjoying how hungry he was to taste her body.

Rapunzel lifted a knee, and he rode a hand over her thigh and held it in place. Teeth pinched her nipple and she tugged on his cock harder, squeezing her fingers tight around his solid girth.

"I want…" she panted, catching her breath and trying to speak again, "I want to taste you again."

He let go, surrendering her body as she allowed the cold air to cut between them. Jasper held his breath and watched as she knelt once more. Hot lips pulled his shaft deep into the wet warmth of her mouth, the tip of his cock riding slowly until met with the narrowing of her throat, tight as she suckled. She bobbed up and down on his shaft, and he leaned hard against the cold wall as his knees grew weak.

Gripping her hair, he pulled her off, forcing her to look up at him. Her mouth laid open, tongue like a red carpet, and he watched his dick slide back between her lips until she gagged. Another tug of her hair and the look on her face and moan told him all he needed to know. Bringing her to her feet once more, he pinned her between him and the brick wall, her ass grinding against his cock like they had done all night on stage. She landed two palms against the brick wall and bent over as his hand rode up the back of her thighs and ass cheeks, gripping them tightly before he flipped the skirt up and over her hip.

"Fuck me, Jasper," she panted, wiggling her ass.

With no panties to stop his fingers from rubbing between her swollen folds, he took his time. Slowly, he dipped a finger inside her, hot and wet, and she pushed into him. Both aching, he abandoned his initial aim to play with her. Jasper gripped Rapunzel's hips and pushed his rock-hard cock inside her dripping pussy. Both hummed with the satisfaction of getting to the main event. He took pleasure in pulling all the way out of her, his dick wet and slick from her. Again, slow and agonizing, enjoying every sensation of entering her over and over again.

Her dreads and braids swayed more as he increased the tempo of his fucking. At last, his hands glided over her hip and returned to groping her breasts. Her pussy tightened and he grunted into her ear.

"Shit, I'm…" His voice added to her arousal, her tightening cutting his words. "…Fuck."

"Cum inside me," she moaned, hands reaching back gripping fistfuls of his shirt.

"But…" his tempo faltered, "I don't have a condom."

"I'm on birth control." She rocked into him. "Now give me what I want." Her demand made his cock throb inside her.

"As you wish, my majesty." His murmur made her shiver. "You've let down your hair … and … I've entered your tower."

"Faster, harder," she moaned.

Groping her breast tightly, he pounded her. Rapunzel's skin pimpled as the heat of his breath washed over her neck and shoulder. The thought at any moment someone could discover them, goading them to the edge, until at last, he peaked. A groan escaped him as he shoved forward firm against her, trapping her between him and the brick wall. She inhaled swiftly, the knowing warmth filling her as his cock jerked with each release of cum inside her. He panted in her ear for a moment, and she let him stay there, pinning her as his lips kissed her neck and shoulder, soft and hot like petals against her skin.

Rapunzel's heart pounded and her knees were weak. *When was the last time someone gave me baby deer legs? That tour in Toronto? Or maybe that comedian in Raleigh?*

"Is this what the naughty girl wanted?" His voice was gruff in her ear as a hand slid down across her abdomen. "Are you going to be a good girl for me?"

"Y-yes." Again, he pressed himself tight against her, his cock still inside her.

A finger rolled over her clit and her pussy tightened on his cock. "Good girl, now cum for me."

He grinded into her, his circling growing more aggressive. "So… so close…"

"Be a good girl. Cum on my cock for me." The rumbling in her ear combined with the hard grope of her breast sent her over the edge.

She moaned, bucking a moment before he pounded her until she screamed in ecstasy. When her legs threatened to give out, he stopped, pulling out slowly and they caught their breaths. She flipped around, still leaning on the wall as the feeling came back to her legs.

"Come back to my place," she begged, unwilling to let this end here.

He laughed, zipping his pants. "Are you sure?"

"Fine, bad boy." She pulled off the wall, throwing her arms around his neck, kissing him before offering, "I've got keys to Bob's place."

"Bob's place?" He blinked and a grin grew on his face. "You got keys to every door in there?"

"Only one way to find out, hmm?" Rapunzel broke away from him, straightened her bra and skirt. "I think we should start with some skinny-dipping and move down to the sex dungeon for more fun?"

"You're taking me places I've never fucked before, and I can't seem to say no," he scoffed.

Honey Cummings

A passionate, award-winning author of Fantasy, Honey has turned her aim towards erotica. Blending everyday scenarios and crafting them into steamy, blood-boiling moments for every shade of audience. Whether you want something short and hot like a student-teacher hook up to the more paranormal flair where Sleep with Sasquatch has unexpected bonus, look forward to erotic short stories, novellas, and hopefully a Trilogy in the future. Honey's debut erotic short landed No. 3 in Urban Erotica and continues to satisfy readers time and time again. Be sure to leave her a review and let her know what you think!

https://www.amazon.com/Honey-Cummings/e/
B07WFX5FDX
www.AuthorHoneyCummings.com
instagram.com/authorhoneycummings
twitter.com/HoneyCummings2
facebook.com/
Author-Honey-Cummings-101408818012749

MORE HONEY CUMMINGS BOOKS

Sleeping with Sasquatch
Cuddling with Chupacabra
Naked with New Jersey Devil
Laying with the Lady in Blue
Wanton Woman in White
Beating it with Bloody Mary

Beau and Professor Bestialora
The Goat's Gruff
Goldie and Her Three Beards
Pied Piper's Pipe

More Books from 4 Horsemen Publications

Erotica

Ali Whippe

Office Hours
Tutoring Center
Athletics
Extra Credit
Financial Aid
Bound for Release
Fetish Circuit
Now You See Him
Sexual Playground
Swingers

Chastity Veldt

Molly in Milwaukee
Irene in Indianapolis
Lydia in Louisville
Natasha in Nashville
Alyssa in Atlanta
Betty in Birmingham
Carrie on Campus

DALIA LANCE

My Home on Whore Island
Slumming It on Slut Street
Training of the Tramp
The Imperfect Perfection
Spring Break
72% Match
It Was Meant To Be... Or Whatever

NOVA EMBERS

A Game of Sales
How Marketing Beats Dick
Certified Public Alpha (CPA)
On the Job Experience
My GIF is Bigger than Your GIF
Power Play
Plugging in My USB
Hunting the White Elephant
Caution: Slippery When Wet

SHAE COON

Bound in Love
Controlling Assets
For His Own Protection
Her Broken Pieces

www.ingramcontent.com/pod-product-compliance
Lightning Source LLC
Chambersburg PA
CBHW050500110726
47899CB00003B/1018